Too Quiet for These Old Bones

by **Tres Seymour**

pictures by **Paul Brett Johnson**

Orchard Books   New York

Orchard Books, 95 Madison Avenue, New York, NY 10016

Manufactured in the United States of America
Printed by Barton Press, Inc.   Bound by Horowitz/Rae
Book design by Jennifer Browne

10 9 8 7 6 5 4 3 2 1

The text of this book is set in 18 point Accolade Light.
The illustrations are acrylic paintings.

Library of Congress Cataloging-in-Publication Data
Seymour, Tres.
Too quiet for these old bones / by Tres Seymour ; pictures by Paul Brett Johnson.
p.   cm.
Summary: When Granny complains that her house is far too quiet, her
four grandchildren are more than happy to help remedy the situation.
ISBN 0-531-30052-8. — ISBN 0-531-33052-4 (lib. bdg.)
[1. Grandmothers—Fiction.   2. Noise—Fiction.   3. Stories in rhyme.]
I. Johnson, Paul Brett, ill.   II. Title.
PZ8.3.S496To   1997   [E]—dc21   96-53301

Granny's house is very quiet.
Silent as a tomb.
We were doomed to spend all Tuesday
in her living room.

The cat purred low, the flies buzzed soft,
dust settled like a snow.
Mom had said that if we made a racket
Granny's nerves would go.

Jane and I and Logan sat
and quietly swung our feet.
Lucas, who is five, had orders
Not To Make A Bleat.

Then something seemed to cut the air,
to slice it like a knife—
Granny, who had been so boring,
came to sudden life.

Granny's back went straight as sticks,
her eyes took on a gleam;
she looked as though she wanted
to let out a healthy scream.

Bang she wanted, bang she'd get.
We took her at her word.
We piled the china on the steps.
An avalanche occurred.

We launched the model rockets
Daddy built when he was young.
Lucas, who is five, made noise
by blibbering with his tongue.

We clacked the mousetraps, slammed the doors,
sang songs till we were blue. . . .
We even played "Hail to the Chief"
on whistle and kazoo.

And Granny said, "My dears,
is *that* the best that you can do?
Back in my day we knew how
to make a decent shout.
You suck in one good gulp of air
and holler it back out!"

Janie wailed a siren's wail.
Logan yodeled loud.
Lucas threw a fit that would have
made a banshee proud.

I cried, "Oh, hallelujah!"
just as hard as I could bawl,
and Granny screamed a screaming whoop,
the loudest of us all.

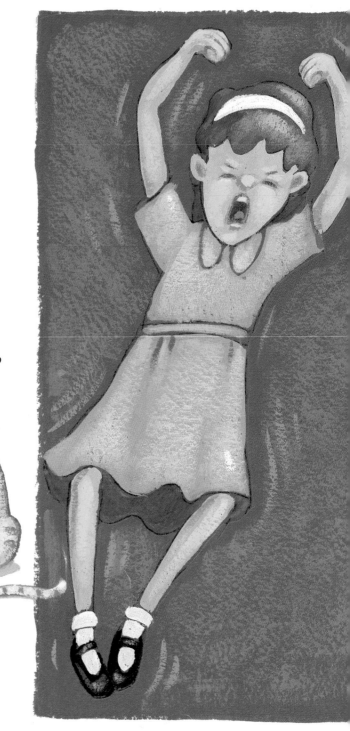

We sounded like a train
   had wrecked—
you wouldn't believe the din—
so loud we didn't hear
   a thing when

Mom came in.

Granny's house is very quiet.
Silent as a tomb.
We have come to spend all Wednesday
in her living room.

The cat purrs low, the flies buzz soft,
dust settles like a snow.

But only till we hear our mom
start up the car and go. . . .